Concrete

By Debbie Croft

Illustrations by Nives Porcellato and Andrew Craig

Contents

How to Make a Concrete Driveway

Goal

To make a concrete driveway.

Materials

- ready-mixed concrete
- timber (for formwork)
- reinforcing mesh
- chairs
- concreting wheelbarrow
- metal rake
- screed
- float
- curing compound
- concrete saw
- hose and water

wheelbarrow

metal ra[ke]

float

chairs

Steps

1. Arrange a suitable delivery time with the company that will be supplying the ready-mixed concrete. Advise them of the size of the area to be concreted, and the type of job to be completed. Concrete mixtures are made up according to the purpose for which the finished concrete will be used.

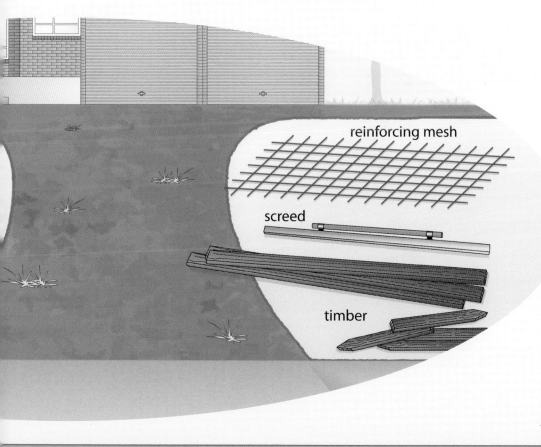

reinforcing mesh

screed

timber

2. Make sure the site has been prepared before the concrete is delivered.

3. Dig out the section where the driveway will be located, allowing at least a 100 mm depth for the concrete. Check that the soil where the concrete will be poured is well-drained and compacted.

4. Set up formwork that will allow the concrete to be positioned in the right place. Install reinforcing mesh to help strengthen the concrete. This mesh will be suspended in the wet concrete on chairs.

chair

5. Have the driver pour the concrete from the chute into a wheelbarrow. Start at the far end of the driveway and tip the concrete into the formwork. With each subsequent load, move back towards the truck. In some places it may be possible to pour the concrete directly from the chute into the formwork.

6. As the formwork is filled with wet concrete, use a metal rake to evenly spread the mix. Then use a long screed to level the concrete. Finish the surface of the concrete with a float in a backwards and forwards arcing motion. This will bring the finer sand and cement particles to the top for a smooth finish.

7. Once satisfied with the finished effect, apply a curing compound or a fine spray of water to the top of the concrete to prevent it from drying too fast. This allows the hydration of the concrete to occur evenly throughout the mix.

8. Because concrete will shrink as it hardens, and to prevent it from cracking, make control joints at even intervals along the driveway. Do this with a concrete saw the day after the concrete has been poured.

Using Concrete in Earthquake Areas

Like all natural disasters, earthquakes can cause considerable damage. Lives may be lost, and buildings and other man-made structures can be ruined. This is why there is often debate about the use of concrete for buildings in earthquake zones.

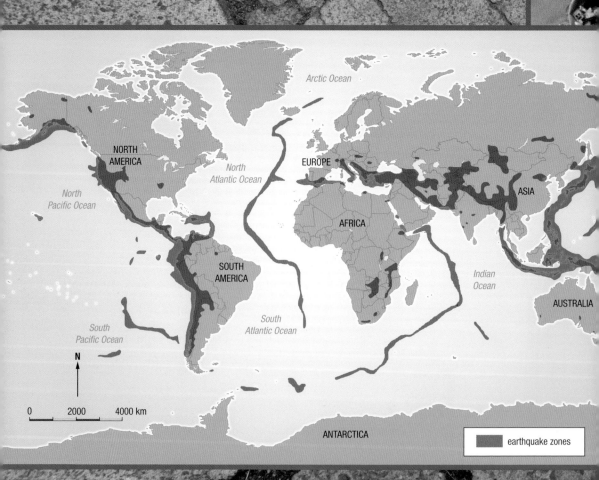

In 2007, this building was destroyed by an earthquake in Osaka, Japan.

Some people are convinced that concrete is safe to use on all building sites, even in areas where the ground can be unstable.

Over the years, engineers have done a lot of research. They have drawn special plans for new buildings, hoping these designs would make the buildings more resistant to earthquakes. In many places, these specially-designed buildings have resisted a greater amount of force when an earthquake occurred.

Building standards have improved and this means concrete can be used more safely. Some of the other benefits of using concrete are that it lasts a long time, it is cheaper than other building materials, and it is less likely to move under normal conditions.

On the other hand, there are some people who strongly object to using concrete for buildings in areas where earthquakes are likely to occur. They believe that people in those communities are more at risk. Footage of earthquake-affected sites show that there would be little chance of survival for people inside a concrete building if it collapsed.

But these are not the only people at risk. There is extreme danger for rescue workers as they search through piles of concrete rubble looking for survivors.

Rescue workers check for earthquake survivors in the Sichuan province, China, 2008.

Other materials such as timber and steel can be used to replace concrete in some buildings. Wood can be used successfully if it is treated so it does not soak up moisture. Steel is strong and is more stable for use in areas that are at risk of earthquakes.

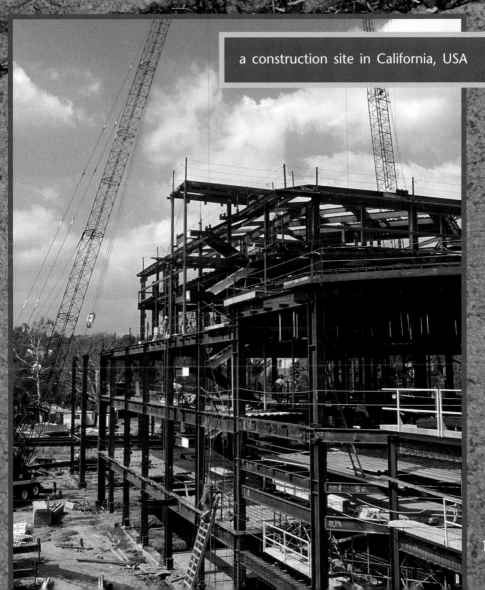

a construction site in California, USA

Knowing that concrete has other advantages means it can be used in buildings all over the world. However, after considering these arguments, it is evident that the risks can be reduced by using less concrete and building earthquake-resistant structures.